As a passionate lover of Irish folklore and an avid artist, I am thrilled to introduce you to my latest creation - an adult coloring book that celebrates the rich and enchanting world of Irish folklore. This beautiful book contains 22 stunning coloring pages, each one a masterpiece waiting to be brought to life with your imagination and creativity.

From the rolling hills of the countryside to the mystical creatures that roam the land, this book takes you on a journey through the timeless tales of Ireland. Each page is painstakingly created with intricate detail, capturing the essence of the stories that have been passed down from generation to generation. Whether you are a seasoned colorist or just starting out, this book is the perfect way to unwind, relax, and unleash your inner artist.

As you turn each page and bring the stories to life with your colors, I hope that you will be transported to a world of magic and wonder, where anything is possible and the impossible becomes reality. So come and join me on this enchanting journey, and let the stories of Irish folklore come alive in a whole new way.

-GRAYSON

Step into the Enchanted Realm of Irish Folklore: This adult coloring book is a celebration of the rich history and legends of Ireland. From the powerful Fairy Queen Aine to the mischievous fairies of the Otherworld, this coloring book brings to life the mystical creatures of Irish folklore. Immerse yourself in this world of wonder and enchantment as you color your way through each page, discovering the magic and beauty of the Irish Otherworld.

Background Information

BANSHEES - HAUNTING AND ETHEREAL, BANSHEES ARE KNOWN AS THE WAILING WOMEN OF IRISH FOLKLORE. THEY ARE BELIEVED TO BE THE SPIRITS OF WOMEN WHO HAVE DIED AND ARE SAID TO FORETELL DEATH BY THEIR MOURNFUL CRIES.

POOKAS - POOKAS ARE MISCHIEVOUS CREATURES WHO LOVE TO PLAY TRICKS ON HUMANS. THEY ARE DEPICTED AS HORSE-LIKE CREATURES WHO CAN TAKE MANY FORMS, INCLUDING THAT OF A GOAT, RABBIT, OR EVEN A HUMAN.

MERROWS - MERROWS ARE SEA-DWELLING CREATURES WHO ARE SAID TO BE THE MERMAIDS OF IRISH FOLKLORE. THEY ARE DEPICTED AS BEAUTIFUL AND SEDUCTIVE, BUT ALSO DANGEROUS TO SAILORS AND FISHERMEN.

GOBLINS - GOBLINS ARE MISCHIEVOUS CREATURES WHO ARE SAID TO LIVE UNDERGROUND AND ARE KNOWN FOR THEIR LOVE OF PRANKS AND TRICKS. THEY ARE DEPICTED AS SMALL AND UGLY, WITH A LOVE FOR ALL THINGS SHINY.

CHANGELINGS - CHANGELINGS ARE CREATURES WHO ARE SAID TO STEAL BABIES AND REPLACE THEM WITH THEIR OWN OFFSPRING. THEY ARE DEPICTED AS HAVING SUPERNATURAL POWERS AND ARE SAID TO BE DIFFICULT TO DETECT.

FAIRY QUEEN AINE: A CAPTIVATING FAIRY QUEEN: IMMERSE YOURSELF IN THE MAGIC OF IRISH FOLKLORE WITH THIS REPRESENTATION OF THE POWERFUL AND BEAUTIFUL FAIRY QUEEN, AINE. WITH HER MASTERY OF MAGIC AND REIGN OVER THE OTHERWORLD, THIS COLORING BOOK IS A TRIBUTE TO THE GRACE AND SPLENDOR OF THE QUEEN. COLOR YOUR WAY TO A REALM OF WONDER AND ENCHANTMENT.

Background Information

THE MORRIGAN - THE MORRIGAN IS A GODDESS OF DEATH, WAR, AND FATE. SHE IS DEPICTED AS A POWERFUL AND FEARSOME CREATURE WHO ISHAVE THE ABILITY TO SHAPE-SHIFT INTO A CROW OR A RAVEN.

THE CAILLEACH - THE CAILLEACH IS A GODDESS OF THE WINTER AND IS SAID TO BRING THE COLD AND SNOW TO THE LAND. SHE IS DEPICTED AS AN OLD AND WRINKLED WOMAN, OFTEN WITH A SHAWL MADE OF ICE.

FAIRIES OF THE IRISH OTHERWORLD: EXPLORE THE MYSTICAL WORLD OF IRISH FOLKLORE WITH THESE ENCHANTING FAIRIES. FROM MISCHIEVOUS PIXIES TO GRACEFUL SYLPHS, THESE MYTHICAL CREATURES EMBODY THE MAGIC AND WONDER OF THE OTHERWORLD. IMMERSE YOURSELF IN THIS FANTASTICAL REALM AND BRING TO LIFE THE CAPTIVATING BEAUTY OF THE FAIRIES THROUGH YOUR COLORING

THE CLURICHAUN - THE CLURICHAUN IS A FAIRY WHO IS KNOWN FOR HIS LOVE OF WINE AND MISCHIEVOUS BEHAVIOR. HE IS DEPICTED AS A SMALL MANWHO IS OFTEN DRUNK AND IS SAID TO LIVE IN WINE CELLARS.

REDCAP: KNOWN FOR HIS BLOODTHIRSTY WAYS, THIS MALEVOLENT IMP SPREADS FEAR WITH HIS SHARP CLAWS AND FIERY TEMPER. COLOR YOUR WAY THROUGH THE SUPERNATURAL AND EXPERIENCE THE FEARSOME POWER OF THE REDCAP

THE BEAN SI - THE BEAN SI IS A FAIRY QUEEN WHO IS SAID TO REIGN OVER THE FAIRY REALM. SHE IS DEPICTED AS A BEAUTIFUL AND POWERFUL FIGURE, WITH A LOVE FOR NATURE AND THE MAGIC OF THE EARTH.

THE POOKA

The blank pages are intentionally left blank in the coloring book to serve a practical purpose. By including a blank page, it helps to prevent ink from bleeding through to the other side, preserving the quality of the designs and creating a better coloring experience for the user. This serves as a reminder that the page was not accidentally left blank, but was included for this purpose

THE MORRIGAN

The blank pages are intentionally left blank in the coloring book to serve a practical purpose. By including a blank page, it helps to prevent ink from bleeding through to the other side, preserving the quality of the designs and creating a better coloring experience for the user. This serves as a reminder that the page was not accidentally left blank, but was included for this purpose

THE MERROW

The blank pages are intentionally left blank in the coloring book to serve a practical purpose. By including a blank page, it helps to prevent ink from bleeding through to the other side, preserving the quality of the designs and creating a better coloring experience for the user. This serves as a reminder that the page was not accidentally left blank, but was included for this purpose

THE LEPRECHAUN

The blank pages are intentionally left blank in the coloring book to serve a practical purpose. By including a blank page, it helps to prevent ink from bleeding through to the other side, preserving the quality of the designs and creating a better coloring experience for the user. This serves as a reminder that the page was not accidentally left blank, but was included for this purpose

AINE - FAIRY QUEEN

The blank pages are intentionally left blank in the coloring book to serve a practical purpose. By including a blank page, it helps to prevent ink from bleeding through to the other side, preserving the quality of the designs and creating a better coloring experience for the user. This serves as a reminder that the page was not accidentally left blank, but was included for this purpose

THE BEAN-SI

The blank pages are intentionally left blank in the coloring book to serve a practical purpose. By including a blank page, it helps to prevent ink from bleeding through to the other side, preserving the quality of the designs and creating a better coloring experience for the user. This serves as a reminder that the page was not accidentally left blank, but was included for this purpose

THE CLURICHAUN

The blank pages are intentionally left blank in the coloring book to serve a practical purpose. By including a blank page, it helps to prevent ink from bleeding through to the other side, preserving the quality of the designs and creating a better coloring experience for the user. This serves as a reminder that the page was not accidentally left blank, but was included for this purpose

THE CAILLEACH

The blank pages are intentionally left blank in the coloring book to serve a practical purpose. By including a blank page, it helps to prevent ink from bleeding through to the other side, preserving the quality of the designs and creating a better coloring experience for the user. This serves as a reminder that the page was not accidentally left blank, but was included for this purpose

CHILDREN OF THE LIR

The blank pages are intentionally left blank in the coloring book to serve a practical purpose. By including a blank page, it helps to prevent ink from bleeding through to the other side, preserving the quality of the designs and creating a better coloring experience for the user. This serves as a reminder that the page was not accidentally left blank, but was included for this purpose

THE BANSHEE

The blank pages are intentionally left blank in the coloring book to serve a practical purpose. By including a blank page, it helps to prevent ink from bleeding through to the other side, preserving the quality of the designs and creating a better coloring experience for the user. This serves as a reminder that the page was not accidentally left blank, but was included for this purpose

THE FAIRY

The blank pages are intentionally left blank in the coloring book to serve a practical purpose. By including a blank page, it helps to prevent ink from bleeding through to the other side, preserving the quality of the designs and creating a better coloring experience for the user. This serves as a reminder that the page was not accidentally left blank, but was included for this purpose

THE RED CAP

The blank pages are intentionally left blank in the coloring book to serve a practical purpose. By including a blank page, it helps to prevent ink from bleeding through to the other side, preserving the quality of the designs and creating a better coloring experience for the user. This serves as a reminder that the page was not accidentally left blank, but was included for this purpose

THE POOKA

The blank pages are intentionally left blank in the coloring book to serve a practical purpose. By including a blank page, it helps to prevent ink from bleeding through to the other side, preserving the quality of the designs and creating a better coloring experience for the user. This serves as a reminder that the page was not accidentally left blank, but was included for this purpose

THE MORRIGAN

The blank pages are intentionally left blank in the coloring book to serve a practical purpose. By including a blank page, it helps to prevent ink from bleeding through to the other side, preserving the quality of the designs and creating a better coloring experience for the user. This serves as a reminder that the page was not accidentally left blank, but was included for this purpose

THE MERROW

The blank pages are intentionally left blank in the coloring book to serve a practical purpose. By including a blank page, it helps to prevent ink from bleeding through to the other side, preserving the quality of the designs and creating a better coloring experience for the user. This serves as a reminder that the page was not accidentally left blank, but was included for this purpose

AINE - THE FAIRY QUEEN

The blank pages are intentionally left blank in the coloring book to serve a practical purpose. By including a blank page, it helps to prevent ink from bleeding through to the other side, preserving the quality of the designs and creating a better coloring experience for the user. This serves as a reminder that the page was not accidentally left blank, but was included for this purpose

THE BEAN SI

The blank pages are intentionally left blank in the coloring book to serve a practical purpose. By including a blank page, it helps to prevent ink from bleeding through to the other side, preserving the quality of the designs and creating a better coloring experience for the user. This serves as a reminder that the page was not accidentally left blank, but was included for this purpose

THE CLURICHAUN

The blank pages are intentionally left blank in the coloring book to serve a practical purpose. By including a blank page, it helps to prevent ink from bleeding through to the other side, preserving the quality of the designs and creating a better coloring experience for the user. This serves as a reminder that the page was not accidentally left blank, but was included for this purpose

THE CAILLEACH

The blank pages are intentionally left blank in the coloring book to serve a practical purpose. By including a blank page, it helps to prevent ink from bleeding through to the other side, preserving the quality of the designs and creating a better coloring experience for the user. This serves as a reminder that the page was not accidentally left blank, but was included for this purpose

THE GOBLIN

The blank pages are intentionally left blank in the coloring book to serve a practical purpose. By including a blank page, it helps to prevent ink from bleeding through to the other side, preserving the quality of the designs and creating a better coloring experience for the user. This serves as a reminder that the page was not accidentally left blank, but was included for this purpose

THE LEPRECHAUN

The blank pages are intentionally left blank in the coloring book to serve a practical purpose. By including a blank page, it helps to prevent ink from bleeding through to the other side, preserving the quality of the designs and creating a better coloring experience for the user. This serves as a reminder that the page was not accidentally left blank, but was included for this purpose

Printed in Great Britain
by Amazon

36079222R00026